# Barbie™ i can be...

# A Zoo Vet

Concept developed for Mattel by Egmont Creative Center
By Freya Woods
Illustrated by TJ Team Graphic

Special thanks to Karolina Hjertonsson, Lone Jochumsen, Emily Kelly,
Claudia Lucarella, Tanya Mann, Julia Phelps, and Sarah Quesenberry

## Random House 🏠 New York

ISBN: 978-0-375-87265-5
www.randomhouse.com/kids   MANUFACTURED IN CHINA   10 9 8 7 6

**B**arbie and her friends Teresa and Nikki are very excited—they are going to help a vet take care of animals at the zoo!

The girls are volunteering for the summer, and they can't wait to start. They love animals!

Barbie, Nikki, and Teresa quickly change their clothes and meet the zoo vet outside her office.

"A vet takes care of animals when they get sick. But it's just as important to keep the healthy animals happy," she explains.

"Here's a list of all the animals that you'll help me with today," the vet continues. "It will be your job to make sure they all have food and water."

"We can do it," Barbie says confidently.

"Great!" says the vet with a smile. "There are a lot of animals, so you'll have to work fast."

The baby koalas are the first animals on the list. The hungry little babies scamper up to the three friends and drink from their bottles.

"So cute!" says Barbie. "Let's stay here and play with these little guys for a while."

Next, the girls head to the Africa exhibit.
Suddenly, a group of visitors drive up in a tour truck.
"Would you pose for some pictures?" asks a lady.
"Sure," replies Teresa. "It's a lot of fun helping a zoo vet!"

After a few photos, Barbie, Nikki, and Teresa go to feed the dolphins. Barbie tosses a ball—and a baby dolphin bounces it right back!

"They want to play catch with us!" says Nikki.

At the elephant enclosure, a baby elephant dips his trunk into a bucket—and sprays water all over Nikki!

"Guess I needed a bath!" Nikki says with a laugh.

But the playful little elephant isn't through yet.
"Watch out, guys!" yells Nikki.
Barbie and Teresa start to run, but it's too late!
The silly little elephant sprays water all over them, too.

Suddenly, Teresa remembers the list the vet gave them!

"Oh, no!" Teresa cries. "It's getting late, and we still have lots of animals to feed. We shouldn't have spent so much time playing!"

"Come on, everyone!" says Barbie. "Let's hurry up and finish."

Barbie, Nikki, and Teresa jump on their bikes and pedal as fast as they can. They quickly feed the hungry parrots.

At the penguin house, the ice is very slippery. "Let's hold hands to keep our balance," suggests Barbie.

"I wish we could stay and have fun," says Nikki with a sigh.

"Me too," replies Barbie. "But the other animals are counting on us to bring their food and water."

The baby pandas are next on the list. The fluffy little creatures happily drink their milk. When the pandas finish, they begin to yawn. "I think it's time for their nap," Teresa says with a giggle.

Next, Barbie, Teresa, and Nikki ride up to the wild bird lake.
"What colorful peacocks and flamingos!" exclaims Nikki.
"Time to fly!" says Barbie after she finishes feeding the birds.

"You girls did a terrific job," the vet says when their work is done.

"We had a great time," says Nikki.

"And I've learned that I can be a zoo vet!" says Barbie.

"Thanks for helping out, Barbie," Raquelle says.

"Cheering with your team made me feel like I *can* be a cheerleader!" Barbie exclaims.

"You *are* a cheerleader," Raquelle replies. "Welcome to the team!"

"That was so cool!" exclaims Nikki after the competition.
"Way to represent our school and bring home the trophy!"

Barbie and the cheerleading team win!

The team makes a pyramid. With a flip, Barbie spins herself into the air—and lands on top of the pyramid! The crowd goes wild!

The competition is super close!

"We've got to wow the judges to win this," Barbie says.

"Let's do the Kick Twist Basket Toss."

"Time to go, girls!" the coach calls to the team.

"Ready? Okay!" shouts Raquelle, starting the first cheer.

Barbie remembers all the steps and doesn't miss a beat!

and stunts.

"Not bad, Barbie!" Raquelle says.

Barbie and the cheerleading team practice their jumps . . .

cheers . . .

Barbie quickly changes her clothes and gets ready to practice.

"Well, the uniform fits," says Raquelle. "But you'll never learn all the moves in time."

"I can do it!" cries Barbie. "Let's get started."

"Show me what you've got!" Raquelle says to Barbie.

Barbie smiles and does a triple flip before landing in a perfect split.

"Not bad," says Raquelle. "Do you think you can learn all our cheers before the competition?"

"I'll do my best!" says Barbie.

*Riiing!* It's Raquelle's cell phone. Britney has called to say she sprained her ankle—and won't be able to cheer for the competition!

"What am I going to do?" Raquelle asks.

Nikki has an idea. "Barbie's a great cheerleader. She can do it!"

"Hi, Raquelle," Nikki says to the captain of the cheerleading squad. "This is my friend Barbie. She's been very busy with her movies, but she'll be trying out for the team when school starts."

"Before it starts, let's visit the squad," Nikki replies as they head into the stadium. "I want to wish Raquelle luck and introduce you to her. You're going to be the best of friends!"

"I am so excited to see the state cheerleading championship!" exclaims Barbie.

# A Cheerleader

By Rebecca Frazer
Illustrated by Kellee Riley

Random House 🏠 New York

Published in the United States by Random House Children's Books, a division of Random House, Inc.,
1745 Broadway, New York, NY 10019, and in Canada by Random House of Canada Limited, Toronto.
No part of this book may be reproduced or copied in any form without permission from the copyright owner.
Random House and the colophon are registered trademarks of Random House, Inc.
Originally published in different form by Random House Children's Books, a division of Random House, Inc., in 2007.
ISBN: 978-0-375-87265-5
www.randomhouse.com/kids    MANUFACTURED IN CHINA    10 9 8 7 6